The Valiant

MW00951620

Book 4: Night Monsters

Mark Mulle

PUBLISHED BY:

Mark Mulle

To be updated on Mark Mulle's books and latest releases, visit markmulle.com

TABLE OF CONTENTS

Day 1

Hello, my dear diary! I'm Boris the wolf, and it's been six months since the last time I wrote here. My life with my family has been great. My wife Susi and my cubs Tasha and Lobo are happier than ever, now that we've defeated the Zombie Leader and got rid of all the Zombie Hordes who attacked the poor villages.

Along with my friends Oopa and Elly, and the human Steve, we've been living a calm and peaceful life in this beautiful world. I've decided to start writing again after this long hiatus because I want to record the good days of my life along with my family and friends!

Day 2

Another day in the castle. As I wrote previously, we've been living together with Steve since our victory over the Zombie Leader. As promised, Steve started building a huge stadium and a park right off the bat, as soon as we returned home. He completed the stadium a month ago and we mainly use it to play around and have some fun together. It is a majestic and good-looking structure; probably the biggest Steve has ever built so far!

Oh by the way diary, Oopa and Elly got married last month! Now they're wolves bound for life, just like me and my dear Susi. Isn't' that great! Our family is more united now than ever!

Day 3

Today, Steve wanted to start building something new. He has completed most of his projects so far and we already have many structures around here. But now, he wants to build a big farm and seek out for other players who could be living in other areas of this world, and offer them the opportunity to live in this beautiful castle.

Speaking of others, I haven't heard of the village leaders in a long time. The last time we visited Hori was a month ago, and he was doing good with his villagers and his brother, Kozu. I wonder how they're doing now. Steve should go pay them a visit some other day.

Day 4

Steve was plowing the land and preparing the terrain to start planting wheat seeds in a large area, when a villager came by.

"Hello, Steve!" He said.

"Oh hi, aren't you one of Hori's villagers?" He said.

"Yes, that's right! Good to see you, Steve!"

"It's good to see you two. So, how are you and the village doing?"

"We're doing well, sir. But Hori sent me here because he wants to talk to you, if it's not much of a bother."

"Well, of course not! It will be my pleasure to meet Hori once again. We'll be there soon!"

The villager left, and Steve went back to the castle to prepare his stuff; diamond tools, armor, weapons, etc. We never know what we're getting ourselves into, so Steve is always very cautious and takes his best gear whenever he goes out.

Day 5

We left the castle this morning, heading to Hori's village. Steve did not want to take all wolves to the trip, because he thought that would be too much of an effort. If things got hectic down there at the village or if we had to go on a different mission, he'd go back and take all wolves to help.

For now, only Oopa and I are coming along. Steve is riding his horse Pegasus, which is very fast and makes our trip shorter. But strangely, on our way to the village, we saw two Creepers and a Spider walking together by the woods. They didn't notice us, and just walked away. Steve didn't understand the reaction of the Creepers and Spider upon seeing us, but ignored them as well. Oopa and I did the same thing too.

Day 6

At the village, we were greeted by our friend Hori, the leader, and his brother Kozu.

"Ah, good to see you all again. Steve, and the wolves Oopa and Boris! Long time no see." Hori said.

"Welcome, guys!" Kozu said.

"It's good to see you too, Hori and Kozu!" Steve said. "I've come as soon as I received your message."

"Sure! Sorry for giving you all the trouble to come back here Steve, but there's something I would like to talk about."

"No worries, Hori. I'm here to help. What's the matter?"

"You see, we've been a bit worried with the night monsters once again…" Hori said.

"They have been acting… strange." Kozu said.

"Night monsters? Are you saying the Zombie hordes are back?"

"Well, not really. The hordes have been defeated for good thanks to you, and they're weak now. But something weird is going on at night, and I've heard the same thing from the other village leaders Kami, Boko and Sole." Hori said.

"Can you explain further what happened?" Steve said.

"I believe you should see it for yourself. It usually happens late at night, around 2 or 3 am." Kozu said.

"Okay, we'll check them out later."

What are they talking about? Why are they concerned with the night monsters aside from the Zombies?

Day 7

Oopa and I were asleep in Hori's house when he and Steve woke up. It was very dark, and they both left the house to meet the other villagers. We got up and followed them, to see what the night monsters were up to.

"Okay, this is the perfect time. Now let's go to the village's entrance and watch the monsters from there." Kozu said.

Everyone gathered by the village's walls, which were built by Steve many months ago to protect them against the Zombie hordes, and we watched the night creatures which were wandering outside.

"Now, look at that! Can you see it, Steve?" Hori said.

There was in fact something weird going on. The creepers, spiders and skeletons were walking together, forming a line, and behaving out of the ordinary. That was confusing to watch, and they didn't seem to follow a specific order on how they are going to line up. They randomly fall into a line.

"That sure is… something." Steve said. "And have they attacked the villages or anything?"

"No… Not yet, but we don't know what they intend to do." Hori said.

"Alright. I should go check the other villages as well, to better understand what's going on."

Steve doesn't know what is happening, and neither do I. Now that most of the Zombies in this world have disappeared when we defeated the Zombie Horde in the past, why are the other monsters behaving like this?

Day 8

We left the village this morning, and headed to Kami's village, the enchanter. This is the closest village to Hori and it is located five miles to the East. Steve wanted to check things out and hear from Kami what he has to report about this incident.

Hori said has communicated with the other three leaders recently, and all three noticed weird events like the one from the previous night: Creepers, Skeletons, Spiders and sometimes even Endermen acting strangely as if they're being controlled by someone or something! This is definitely something we need to investigate.

Day 9

We arrived in the next village late at night, but fortunately Kami was still awake.

"Steve and the wolves! Glad to see you all."

"Hello Kami, it's great to be back." Steve said.

"Thanks for coming, Steve. I believe I know why you are here. Hori, already told you that the other villagers are experiencing the same phenomenon his village is experiencing, isn't he?

"Yes, he did. He and his villagers showed me how the monsters have gone crazy. I'm here to check how your village is doing."

"We're doing fine, thanks to the walls you built as a protection for the Zombie hordes. In fact, we have not been attacked ever since

16

the Zombie Hordes have been defeated, but I can't tell for sure what the other monsters are up to."

"I see. Well, have you talked with the other two leaders? What did they say?"

"Sole and Boko said the same thing. Night monsters going nuts, walking around, forming groups, but disappearing by the morning."

"Okay. I think we need to discuss this together. Can you send them both a letter, asking them to meet us up at Hori's? Let's reunite everyone to talk about this."

"Sure thing, I'll send my best messengers right away." Kami said.

Steve has called in for a meeting with all village leaders. It's the best thing they can do at this moment: to sit and discuss the subject. Maybe they can find a clue of what's going on.

Day 10

We returned to Hori's village the following day, where we'd wait for the other three leaders for the meeting. I don't know for sure what Steve has in mind, if he's got a plan himself or if he just wants to talk.

But what really remains a mystery here is, why are the night monsters respawning so fast even after the Dragon's defeat? They have been weak for months, and suddenly they return to their normal spawn rate? No wonder everyone is worried, this might mean the Zombie hordes could be on their way, and that's the last thing we want to happen.

Day 11

At Hori's village, Steve talked with Hori and Kozu about the meeting. They liked the idea of having a meeting with all village leaders and discuss new plans to deal with this potential threat.

"Do you think it will be Hordes attacking villages all over again?" Oopa asked me.

"I don't know, but I sure hope it's not." I said.

While the other villagers haven'tarrived yet, Steve decided to build a small inn within the village with rooms enough to accommodate all leaders once everyone was here.

At night, we watched the night monsters wandering in the woods from the village's walls. The same thing happened from before – night monsters forming lines, and walking back and forth to the woods.

Day 12

Kami and Sole arrived this morning. Boko was still on his way. The three leaders and Steve convened at the town hall to talk about the night creatures.

"This is an unprecedented event, but we might be looking at something similar to what happened when the Zombies attacked." Kami said.

"It's a tough situation. We don't know what we are dealing with." Hori said.

"I'd love to help and provide as much info as possible of my days as the Zombie Leader... But too bad I lost most of my memories." Kozu said.

Kozu was once taken by the Zombie Horde.

"Don't blame yourself, Kozu." Steve

said. "You were under the Zombie's control. As for the night monsters, I don't have any concrete plans for now, but I was thinking I should strike them with my wolves to see what happens."

"Strike them? As in, attack?" Hori said.

"Yes. Oopa and Boris are brave and strong. My horse Pegasus is equipped with Diamond armor, and I've got my full enchanted Diamond set. Together, we are invincible! I'd like to see the monsters' reactions when attacked. This could lead us somewhere. I think…"

"I don't know if it's a good idea, but we don't have any others. So I guess you should do it, Steve." Hori said.

The others agreed. We're going to attack the night monsters the next time we see them doing what was agreed upon.

Day 13

It was late at night when we left the village. Steve got on Pegasus and we followed them. The other villagers stayed behind and watched us from the walls.

"Alright, Boris and Oopa, it's time for some action!" Steve said.

"Let's do it, guys!" I said.

"Yeah, it's going to be easy." Oopa said.

We entered the woods and searched for the monsters. We did not find any.

"Weird... they should've spawned by now." I said.

Steve saw a Skeleton going further into the woods and rushed at him. We followed him, and in a clearing at the forest, we found them; Creepers, Skeletons, and Spiders, forming a circle and walking around. They didn't even notice us!

"Alright guys, attack!" Steve said.

Oopa and I jumped on a Skeleton. Steve attacked some Creepers. We easily got rid of them, but the others didn't move an inch. They continued doing whatever they were doing.

"What is going on? Let's attack the others!" Steve said.

We assailed the others and just like before, the monsters did not counter attack, and acted as if nothing happened. After defeating all monsters, we returned to the village and Steve reported the incident. Everyone was confused about what happened... What, or who could be controlling those monsters? Why are they behaving like that?

Day 14

Today, the last village leader Boko arrived.

"Sorry for getting here so late, everyone. But something happened back there at the village."

"What is it, Boko?" Hori asked.

"The night monsters attacked the walls! Good thing Steve built the walls before with reinforced layers so they weren't able to enter the village, but it was pretty scary."Boko said. "That's why I was late."

"What? The night monsters, as in Spiders, Skeletons and Creepers?" Steve asked him.

"Yes, all of them except Zombies."

"That is... unbelievable." Steve said.

The three leaders narrated to Boko what happened when Steve, Oopa and I attacked the monsters last night. He was equally disturbed with the facts. How come the creatures attacked his village but simply ignore Steve's presence and action here? More importantly, why did the monsters attack Boko's village and not the other villages?! That's what a Zombie would do, but not the others!

"Do you think there is another leader controlling the monsters just like what happened with the Zombie Horde?" asked Hori.

"Who could be that leader?" Boko said.

They discussed all day long about the facts and the possibilities, without reaching any consensus on what to do next.

"This is bad, Oopa." I said. "I guess we should go get the others to help."

"You're right, let's try to convince Steve to go back home." Oopa said.

Whatever happens next, we should be prepared.

Day 15

Oopa and I tried to talk Steve into going back home. We usually jump around and bark at him when we want him to do something.

"What is it, guys? You two seem worried." Steve said.

We continue jumping around and barking.

"Yes, I am worried with this situation as well."

We ran away from him and barked once more.

"Oh, you want to bring the other?"

We came back and sit next to him.

"Alright, you want to go home and take the others. Isn't that right? Okay, you two are very smart. I got to agree, it would be better to have some reinforcements by our side. Elly and Susi are adults and can handle the heat, and even Tasha and Lobo have grown up enough to deal with the monsters. I'll tell Hori we're going home and we'll be back with the others in no time."

Great, we were able to convince Steve to go home! Having everyone working together should be safer for both us and our family; we left the village in the afternoon.

Day 16

Going back home, we talked about how it was important to reunite everyone for this mission. Although we don't know what we are dealing with, we could use some help from the other wolves.

Steve is aware of this, and he doesn't want to take any risks. The monsters might start forming hordes once again, like they did at Boko's village.

Day 17

Home, sweet home. We got to our beloved family and castle this morning. We happily cheered each other. After telling everyone what happened the previous days, they were glad we actually came back for them.

"Alright. If Steve and the others need our help, we'll gladly join you." Susi said.

"That's right. We've defeated the Zombies once; we can do this against the other monsters!" Elly said.

"Dad, are we also coming along?" Tasha asked me.

"Of course, sweety! You and your brother are part of this team, and we need you now more than ever. Together, we are an invincible team!"

"Yay! I'll help too, dad!" Lobo said.

Steve packed up more items and tools for our return to Hori's village, and he's also taking some extra weapons to distribute to the villagers. We don't know what we are up to, but we sure know we're facing them with everything we've got!

Day 18

Now that we have the crew with us, we're going back to Hori's village to further assist them in discovering what is going on with the monsters. Steve mounted Pegasus as usual, and we're following him.

"Honey, what if the monsters are being controlled by some other leader, just like with the Zombies?" Susi said.

"That's what we thought, Susi. The villagers believe this could be the case. No matter what it is, we haven't confirmed anything yet."

"Okay. Let's help them as much as we can."

That's right. We will do our best. I am sure we will succeed, just like before.

Day 19

We got to the village. But strangely enough, the village no longer had walls! At first sight, it seemed someone had removed the walls. But upon closer inspection, as we approached the village, we realized it had been blown up!

"Steve, thank goodness you're back!" Hori said. "You won't believe it – the night monsters attacked us last night!"

"What? How come?" He asked him.

"Yes, I know this sounds crazy. But look at the wall – the entire South and East walls have been destroyed by Creepers! They came towards the walls and blew up, as if they wanted to destroy it by themselves!"

"That's terrifying… Creepers acting on their own, blowing up walls? That's some serious stuff. Anyway, I'll get to work right away to build up a new wall. The rest of you, stay inside and keep the village on watch."

As Steve rebuilt the wall, we split up and covered different areas of the village. Fortunately, the night monsters don't spawn during the day, so we had no trouble at all. Earlier this evening, Steve finished building the new Rock wall. He doubled the layers this time, to hold off against Creepers.

Regardless of our actions, we need to find out why the Creepers attacked. This is our priority right now.

Day 20

Nothing bad happened last night. In fact, no monsters showed up. Everyone at the village was relieved.

"Good relief. I didn't sleep at all last night." Kami said.

"Me neither." Boko said. "By the way, I'm afraid we'll have to return to our villages right away. What if the monsters are attacking them too?!"

"Don't worry, Boko." Steve said. "I'll visit the other villages with Pegasus and I will rebuild the walls, to make it stronger. It's the least we can do right now. You guys can stay here and discuss a new plan to counterattack the monsters."

"Are you sure, Steve?" Hori said.

"Yes, I'm the only one who can build

the walls, and we need your thinking heads to come up with a plan. We'll be good!"

"Alright, thanks in advance." Sole said. "We'll work together to reach a consensus then."

"Oopa and Elly, come with me. Boris and his family stay here and protect the village." Steve said.

"Alright. Stay safe, guys, and good luck!" I told Oopa and Elly.

"Thanks, you too!" Oopa said.

Steve left the village with Pegasus, Oopa and Elly. They're on their way to secure the other villages. As for us, we'll stay put and help the village leaders with their needs.

Day 21

Now that we're left to take care of Hori's village, my family and I have been working together to protect the good people here. It's very nice to be by their side. Susi and the kids have been happy to be back in action, and so did I.

The leaders reunited once again to talk about the night monsters. I stayed by Hori's side during the meeting to understand what was going on.

"So, we all know the night monsters have been working together to take us down. This is a fact by now, considering the attacks from the previous day." Hori said. "What is our next step?"

"Steve is working hard to protect us right now. That should count as our first step. Now, we need to do something else – and fast."

Kami said.

"I can't help but think there might be someone behind this." Boko said. "Why would the night monsters go on a rampage by themselves?"

"That's what I have been thinking." Sole said. "It's hard to believe they decided to attack out of the blue."

"Alright. So let's assume the monsters have one leader, or even more leaders behind them." Hori said. "Where could we find those leaders?"

No one had a clue. But Kozu spoke up:

"Hey. I know this is just a guess, a total shot in the dark, but… wasn't the Dragon Egg destroyed in The End?"

"Huh… No, the Egg was not destroyed according to Steve." Hori said.

"Well…" Kami said. "What do you guys think?"

The leaders didn't want to consider this possibility, but everyone knew what they had in mind: what if someone stole the Egg and, somehow, gained control over the monsters? Or even, used it to respawn a new Ender Dragon?

"At this point, we must take all options." Kozu said.

"And what do we do about it?" Sole said.

"Investigate. We need to go back to The End." Kozu said.

Now, we should return to The End with Steve and see if the Egg was still there.

Day 22

With a new plan in mind, the leaders have been gathering items and preparing everything for a new trip. Steve is the only person who can go to The End, so it's only natural we'll have to wait for him to come back from the other villages. It should not take longer than three or four days from now.

The leaders prepared a few maps, leading to The End's portal location. Hori still remembered where the portal was located. He drew it himself while the others picked up food, tools and weapons for the trip. Hori still had the horse that Steve tamed for him, so he'd use it to transport the items.

All we have to do now is make sure the village is safe, and wait for Steve and the wolves to return. Once he is here, we'll go to The End once again, and Steve will check if the Egg is still there. If it is, the Egg must be destroyed.

Day 23

Another peaceful day by the village. The leaders still gather around to talk and discuss new plans and ideas, but they have not come up with anything else better than the plan of the previous day.

Tasha and Lobo have been having a blast here. They patrol the village every day, from north to south and west to east. The villagers have grown fond of them, and they call them the "Wolf Duo".

Susi and I spend most of our days following Hori. When Steve's not around, we feel really comfortable by his side. To be fair, everyone here in this village is trustworthy, but we've known Hori for a long time and he likes us just as much.

Anyway, so far so good diary! When

Steve is here, we'll go to The End and get rid of that Egg. If it is still there…

Day 24

And just when we thought the bad days were over…

The monsters came at night and assailed the village again! And not only that, but they performed an extremely well-coordinated attack!

First, we heard explosions coming from the walls. Everyone woke up in the middle of the night. We knew those were the Creepers again, but fortunately Steve made a sturdy and resistant wall.

When the Creepers stopped blowing up the wall, the Spider Jockeys climbed the walls! They are dangerous mobs, because the Spider can climb structures and the Skeleton shoots his arrows at the enemies.

When the Spider Jockeys entered the

village, my family and I attacked them. Too bad for the Jockeys we are a strong and talented team, with a vast experience with bones and such! Getting rid of the Skeletons was easy. Tasha and Lobo had fun at it. Susi and I covered them. Then, we deal with the pesky Spiders which tried to get away and return to the outside of the wall.

After taking care of the six or seven Jockeys who came inside, we heard new Creepers blowing up from the outside of the wall. A few explosions later, they retreated with the other Spiders and Skeletons who were waiting next to them.

In short, the attack consisted of Creepers trying to take down the walls, and Spider Jockeys climbing and getting inside the village to attack the innocent villagers. Thanks to our group attack, we managed to restrain the attackers and keep everyone safe. Good thing I brought my family to the battlefield!

The villagers were thankful for having us. But we need Steve now more than ever! The walls have sustained heavy damage, and holes began to appear. The walls might not last one more attack like this one.

Day 25

Another day, and no signs of Steve and the wolves. The villagers were getting really worried, because we would not be able to handle monsters coming everywhere after the walls had been taken down.

"If Steve does not return tomorrow, we need to send one of the wolves to go after him. I guess Boris may track him down using his nose." Hori said.

I barked and sat next to him. I agree Hori; I will go after Steve if he doesn't show up soon. We need his help, and we need to find the Egg immediately and have it destroyed. This might end the attacks from the night monsters.

Day 26

It was about 4pm in the afternoon, and still nothing from Steve. Hori opened the village's main gate and I followed him outside.

"Sorry to ask you to do something like this, Boris." Hori said. "But unfortunately we can no longer wait. You'll have to go find Steve for us."

I agreed. Maybe he ran into trouble in the other villages as well, so that's why he is taking so long to return to Hori's village. And right when I was about to leave the place, we saw Steve mounting Pegasus in the horizon.

"Hello there!" He yelled, with Elly and Oopa right next to him.

"Oh thank goodness, Steve is back!" Hori said.

I ran towards them and gave them a warm welcome. Elly and Oopa were happy to see me too. Steve rode to the village and greeted all the villagers and the leaders. After settling down, the leaders invited Steve for a meeting, to explain their current plan.

"So you guys want to go to The End and see if the Egg is still there? Because the Egg might have given birth to a new Dragon, or even worse… some creature might have taken it away?" Steve said.

"Well, we don't know what to make of it." Boko said. "But this is the best we can do now."

"Sounds good. I'm on it!" Steve said. "When are we leaving?"

"As soon as possible." Hori said. "We've made the arrangements; we'd like you to check if they're of your liking."

Steve and the leaders are getting ready for the trip. And we, the wolves, will be by their side in this journey.

Day 27

We departed for The End's portal. The group consisted of Steve and Pegasus, Hori and his horse (which he hasn't given a name yet), and us wolves. The three village leaders and Hori's brother, Kozu, stayed behind, because we thought it would be dangerous to take too many villagers with us.

Besides, we don't have a horse for everyone. Us wolves can easily catch up with Steve's and Hori's horses, but the leaders can't.

"We wish you good luck." Boko said. "Our hopes are with your group!"

"Have a safe trip!" Kami said.

"Thanks everyone. We'll be right back with the news! And may they be good news for us." Steve said.

We're following Hori's map, which

indicates the exact position of the portal. It's not far from the villages, but it is in the middle of nowhere. At least we have a map, which is better than picking up Ender Pearls and throwing them around!

Day 28

On our journey to The End once again, we remembered everything from the time we found the Portal – how we had to protect the entrance while Steve slayed the Dragon, and how the Zombies would not stop spawning.

Now, we had a different reason to go: even though most of the Zombies had completely disappeared, the other monsters got stronger and independent. What if Steve finds a new Dragon waiting for him in The End? One that hatched from the Egg?

Who knows what could happen.

Day 29

Not long after our departure, we reached the spot known as the End Portal's location. The area still had the holes we dug to get to the portal, which was underground. Steve placed stairs and dug a bigger hole, and we came down.

At The End's entrance, we wished Steve good luck, and stayed behind to protect the portal while he entered The End once again.

Just like before, we stayed on watch and did our best to help Steve. But unlike our previous watch, we had zero monsters coming at us. Exactly zero. None. No Zombies, Creepers, Skeletons or Spiders. What gives?

At least Steve is in there. Let's just wait for him to come out!

Day 30

Steve came out of the portal this morning. He was sweating and extremely anxious.

"The End has… The End has gone crazy!" He said.

"What happened, Steve?" Hori asked him.

"That place was crazy! The gravity was totally off – I could barely stand on my feet, and it was very hard to walk around."

"What else happened?"

"The Egg… The Egg was not there!" He said.

Bingo. Just like we expect (or didn't expect), the Egg was gone.

"We need more details, Steve. What else did you see?" Hori asked him.

"Well, it's more like what I DIDN'T see. You know what is super weird? The Endermen have disappeared. Gone! Poof!"

"What? But The End is their home! Why would they…"

"I don't know Hori, but something fishy is going on. The End is no longer a normal place. The Endermen don't live there anymore, and the Egg has been stolen."

"But if only humans can enter in The End…" Hori said. "Then who…"

"I don't know, buddy. I don't know."

This is a big revelation. The Dragon Egg does have something to do with all of these attacks. More importantly, who took the Egg from The End?

Day 31

Returning to the village, we were unsure of how to proceed next. Steve is thinking about who could have entered The End and grabbed the Egg. And even if we knew who did it, why is the Dragon Egg so important? Is this person using the Dragon Egg to control the other night monsters?

We're going to report everything we know to the village leaders. Now that their villages have received stronger walls to hold off the attacks, they will have more time to think. But time is not by our side – and the holder of the Dragon Egg has the drop on us.

We need to work together now more than ever. Finding the Egg is our priority, because it might lead to who or what is controlling the night monsters who have gone crazy.

If the time comes, my dear diary, we might have to deal with monster hordes once again. But these are not ordinary Zombie hordes; they're hordes of all monsters, united! It will be a tough task, but one we can surely get through working as a big team and as a family.

The Ender Dragon Egg is missing!

Steve went back to the End only to discover that the Dragon Egg is missing. Can this be the reason why the night monsters are acting strangely, spawning in great numbers and relentlessly attacking the villagers? Is the leader of the night monsters the one who also stole the egg of the Ender Dragon?

Join Steve and his pack of wolves lead by Boris as they go on a mission not only to discover who stole the Ender Dragon Egg but also identify the leader of the night monster while protecting the villages from the incoming attacks.

Read The Valiant Wolf Diaries, Book 5: Back to the End for the continuation of Boris and Steve's adventures!

Made in the USA
Coppell, TX
21 March 2022

75319215R00033